Someday, Narwhal

WRITTEN BY
Lisa Mantchev

ILLUSTRATED BY
Hyewon Yum

A Paula Wiseman Book
Simon & Schuster Books for Young Readers
New York London Toronto Sydney New Delhi

Someday, Narwhal

For Phil Boynton, who opened doors for so many, with my love
—L. M.

To my friends, who get me out the door
—H. Y.

SIMON & SCHUSTER BOOKS FOR YOUNG READERS
An imprint of Simon & Schuster Children's Publishing Division
1230 Avenue of the Americas, New York, New York 10020
Text copyright © 2017 by Lisa Mantchev
Illustrations copyright © 2017 by Hyewon Yum
SIMON & SCHUSTER BOOKS FOR YOUNG READERS is a trademark of Simon & Schuster, Inc.
For information about special discounts for bulk purchases, please contact Simon & Schuster Special Sales
at 1-866-506-1949 or business@simonandschuster.com.
The Simon & Schuster Speakers Bureau can bring authors to your live event. For more information or to book an event,
contact the Simon & Schuster Speakers Bureau at 1-866-248-3049 or visit our website at www.simonspeakers.com.
Book design by Laurent Linn
The text for this book was set in Cabrito.
The illustrations for this book were rendered in colored pencils and gouache.
Manufactured in China
0717 SCP
First Edition
2 4 6 8 10 9 7 5 3 1
CIP data for this book is available from the Library of Congress.
ISBN 978-1-4814-7970-7
ISBN 978-1-4814-7971-4 (eBook)

The world doesn't look very exciting from inside a fishbowl.

Red front door.

Potted plant.

Umbrella stand.

Piano.

Red front door.

Potted plant.

Umbrella stand.

Piano.

There's also the window, with a square of bright, blue sky.

The view doesn't change much,
but little narwhals who live in
fishbowls have a lot of dreams.

"Someday, I'm going to travel everywhere.

Someday, I'm going to see the world!"

But then the narwhal thinks about how she hasn't any feet.

She doesn't know any of the street names.

And what if it's cold outside?

"I should just stay home where it's warm."

Red front door.

Potted plant.

Umbrella stand.

Piano.

One day the boy opens the red front door.

His friends have come to play.

"I worry that it's boring for her,
stuck in this bowl," the boy says.

"It *is* a little boring," the narwhal admits.

"Someday, I would like to see the world."

"But I haven't any feet."

"We could help you see the world,"
says the bat.

"We can roll you about the neighborhood," the penguin says.

"I will be very careful with you, just as if you were my egg."

"But I don't know any of the street names,"
the narwhal says.

"I'll help with that," says the giraffe.

"I can read all the signs from up here."

Looking around the room, the narwhal realizes that she is *very* good at memorizing things.

"If you read the signs to me, I can learn the street names as we go. That way we can't get lost."

"But what if it's too cold outside?" she suddenly remembers.

The bat looks out the window at that perfect square of blue. "Not a cloud in the sky," he says.

The narwhal takes a big, brave breath. "Someday is today," she says. "Let's go see the world."

The children run along.

The bat flies along.

The penguin toddles along.

The giraffe marches along.

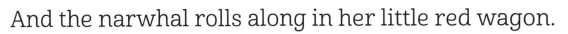

And the narwhal rolls along in her little red wagon.

Down the sidewalk they go, and oh,
there's so much to see! There's the flower shop
and the bookstore and the blinking traffic lights!

Buildings and bridges and the big, blue sky!
So much bigger and bluer than the narwhal
ever dreamed when looking out the window.

Big Ben, Eiffel Tower, Great Wall of China, Pyramids.

The whole world can be her fishbowl.